Grandfat Stories

by Pratima Mitchell

Illustrated by Marie Louise Corner

Fife Council Education Department
King's Road Primary School
King's Crescent, Rosyth KY11 2RS

Chapter One
Arson at the Allotment

I was almost home when I remembered my lunch box. I crossed at the pedestrian crossing and tipped my neglected lunch into the litter bin next to the bus stop. Grandmother had packed potato *parathas,* which are delicious but a bit greasy. But then there had been hockey practice, and you can't shove a potato *paratha* down your throat just like that.

A man lounging in the bus shelter caught my eye and grinned, but no one else saw. Just in time. I'd barely crammed my lunch box back into my school bag when I caught sight of Grandfather cycling up the High Street towards me. You couldn't mistake him: beetroot coloured turban, pedalling along nice and easy, with his size eleven feet sticking out like a duck out for a jaunt in a rowing boat. Plastic bags dangled

from each handlebar, so he was on his way home from his allotment. Crammed into my little sister Minnie's old passenger seat was a cardboard box full of vegetables for our tea.

As he sailed up I could see his face wreathed in white hair, smiling his slightly dotty smile; the kind of smile you see on people's faces when their mind is somewhere else. A half-beam smile, the mouth a little open, corners turned up. He puffed his cheeks and blew out, pooh, pooh, as though he had run a marathon. Sometimes he whistled quietly to himself. He was always happy, always interested in everyone – like now when he lifted a hand to wave to someone on the other side of the street.

In that very instant, a white police car overtook him and drew up smartly a little way ahead. To my horror I saw four policemen jump out and stop my grandfather as he tried to pull over to overtake them. I dropped my bag and bike. "Watch these a minute," I shouted to the grinner, and ran as fast as I could to help Grandfather.

"Sorry sir," one of them was saying, "but we have to ask you a few questions." Another was speaking into his radio. "Suspect intercepted at junction of High Street and Middleton Road. Initial questioning and search proceeding. Over." A third was asking, "Can I examine your bags, sir?"

Some people had straggled up to where the action was. Grandfather addressed himself half to them and half to the policemen. "Is it April Fool's Day, officer? Have I robbed a bank or are you stopping me for speeding on my bike? Look, you can see I'm going home from my allotment."

"Hey, Jarnail Singhji! Do you need any help?" Mr Patel from Lovely Department Store shouted. The policemen were digging around in a methodical way among the curly kale and sprouting broccoli. After several dogged tries, one seemed to have found something. He gingerly upturned a plastic bag on the pavement. Out fell a black gun with bits of green stuff sticking to it. I stared in amazement. I didn't think Grandfather had it in him.

"What's this, then?" the policeman said sarcastically, picking it up with one finger. But we could see it wasn't a real gun at all, just a cleverly made plastic toy. Grandfather started to laugh and so did the bystanders, at first nervously and then with great guffaws. "Heh heh," wheezed Grandfather. "You think I've been trading in AK47s down in my cabbages? Heh, heh." Everyone roared. There were a few muted boos. The policemen choked and spluttered and went bright red. "That's a spud gun, officer," said Grandfather in a patient voice. "I bought it for 50p from Mrs de Vine. It was going to be a surprise for my grandson." Everyone turned and stared at me, which was a horrible feeling.

The next day it was all in the local paper. "Bobbies' Boob Wastes Taxpayers' Money" and a picture of Grandfather smiling broadly. Nothing about taking the police to the race relations board or complaining to our M.P. Grandfather's too good-natured for that. It was just a joke for him. He never stays angry for long.

He must be the most popular man on our side of town. He knows everybody and tries to help everyone in all kinds of ways. He'll look after Jenny next-door's baby, or come into school to fix a broken door or mend the sink. Or if Mr Patel has to go to the dentist, Grandfather is called upon to mind Lovely Department Store (it's only a midget corner shop) and he always says yes. You see him all over the place, all six feet of him; and his bright turban gives him even greater height. He marches rather than walks, swinging his long arms as if he's on a parade ground.

Before he came to England with my grandmother, he was in the army and after that he was a master carpenter. Now he's retired and spends almost all his time on his allotment.

There's a whole colony of these allotment freaks down there. Some of them are his friends but one or two of the freaks enjoy being poisonously unfriendly. There's a lot of jealousy about who grows the biggest marrows and onions, and bags first prize in the South Eastern Allotment Growers' Co-operative Annual Fruit, Vegetable and Flower Show. Mr Khruschev and Mr Porcini will do almost anything to sabotage their rivals and Grandfather is definitely Rival Number One. I think it was Mr Khruschev who tipped off the police about the spud gun. He's got the allotment next to Grandfather's and he must have been snooping around when he did a deal with Theo de Vine whose son used to own the spud gun.

In case you don't know, a spud gun's for firing spud pellets with. It's completely harmless, but it could pass for the real thing if you have trouble seeing reality.

It was Theo who rang up the night Percy Pollit's shed burnt down. Grandfather was sitting in the kitchen checking a seed catalogue and making notes with a stubby pencil which lives permanently in his pocket. I like reading his catalogues. Vegetables have the weirdest names: Ailsa Craig onions, Loch Ness stringless beans, Bedford Fillabasket Brussel sprouts, Savoy Best of All cabbages. Their descriptions are all poetical: "Deservedly famous, reliable, wrinkled pea. It produces great crops of rich, sweet green peas in pointed 3-inch pods. Exquisitely sweet and juicy, ideal for freezing and borne on the vine in pairs." Or, "A unique variety of mini-pumpkin. To make individual servings just scoop out the flesh, steam or bake, refill and serve smothered with butter or brown sugar." "Got that, got that," he was muttering as he licked his index finger while turning the pages of brightly-coloured pictures.

Grandmother was into one of her monologues. "So I told Harbans, if you're going to let your wife go to work, then this is what you get. There's Guddi prancing around in mini-skirts and Bobby playing with his Gameboy day and night when he should be doing his homework. I told him, you may be prospering like a king, but this is the price you have to pay." Uncle Harbans is a dentist. It's a sore point with my grandmother that Aunty Jeeti works long hours. Well, so does my mum, who's a nurse, but the difference is she doesn't have a choice. I don't have a dad. Aunty Jeeti doesn't have to go to work, but she wants to.

Grandfather's response was to suck his pencil and look busy.

The phone rang. "Where's your grandfather?" People are always asking that. It was Theo squawking on the line. He took the receiver.

"Oh dear, oh dear. Very sad. Poor PeeWee. We must do everything we can to help him." There was more agitated squawking. Grandmother gave the peas and potato curry the most tactful of stirs while she tried to listen in and figure out what was going on. Finally Grandfather put down the receiver and, fielding her questions before they could start rolling, explained that someone had set fire to Percy's shed last night. Theo had discovered it by chance. She'd gone home, then realised that she'd left her house keys in her shed, walked back to the allotments and found Percy's shed in flames.

Grandmother tucked her *dupatta* behind her ears, rolled up her sleeves and pursed her mouth as if to say, "Well I told you so; they're a bad lot down there, but nobody listens to me."

Grandfather and I went to have a look at the damage after supper. Percy's shed was still smoking. It was nearly dark but you could see bits of glass from the shed window winking on the path, in the black churned-up earth and from the new growth of nettles. Percy's shed had no roof any more. Its wooden walls were charred and bitten into the grain like welts in crocodile skin. Bags of Growmore plant food, bonemeal and fungicide lay scattered all over the ground. Percy's careful order and organisation had been destroyed. It was a war zone.

Grandfather's shed was singed, the window smashed and a couple of soft-fruit bushes upturned, but nothing more serious than that. They must have stopped at this point, possibly because they heard Theo coming back. Even so, they had managed to splodge white paint down one side of the shed. It looked like

"SMASH". Was it an advert for mashed potatoes or a mean threat?

PeeWee was limping around like a sailor who's lost his bearings. He picked up bits of debris in a distracted way. "Dunno why they

gotta pick on me." He blinked rapidly behind his beer-bottle thick glasses, his moon-shaped face even more creased and bewildered-looking than usual. PeeWee was simple and the allotment was his life. He lived with his mother a few houses down from us in Lyons Terrace. You'd see him hobbling to the shops with a list, muttering as he went "Packet of sugar, Red Lion teabags, not Lipton, pound of sausages, one Mighty White" like a mantra. Then he'd limp into Lovely Department Store, shiny-faced and pathetically eager and over-polite. "Oh, yes please, yes please, if it isn't any trouble thank you. Thank you ever so much." People called him Poor Percy until suddenly one day he said, bobbing and bowing, but quite firmly, "Would you mind very much calling me PeeWee." I don't know where he got the name from, but it was better than Poor Percy. Mrs Murdoch in number 15 said he'd been dropped on his head when he was a baby. She told Grandmother, "His ma's a wicked old thing. Got to watch her or she'll put a blight on your potatoes, she will." And it's true, PeeWee's mum really did look weird with her long chin and suspicious, watery blue eyes. On one cheek she had a mole with long white whiskers growing out of it.

Grandfather stepped carefully through the mess. There was a smell of burning rubber in the air. Burning rubber and something else. I sniffed and followed my nose to the back of the sheds and looked into the ditch that ran along the hedge bordering the allotments. I nearly gagged; two half-barbecued rabbits lay in the ditch pleading with me with their lifeless, sightless gaze. They must have been snacking on carrot-tops and got caught in the blaze. But no, their hind legs were bound together with twine. Surely they hadn't been burnt alive? I shivered and felt sick. A patch of undamaged fur trembled in the breeze.

Which maniac would kill two harmless little animals like that, roast them alive, and savagely destroy PeeWee's allotment?

"Me tools 'ave all gone, too. Pinched. 'Ow am I goin' to manage now? And them parsnips and carrots coming along so nicely too, Mr Singh." PeeWee held up his hands together in front of him like a child.

Theo walked up and I took her to the dead animals. She looked horrified but didn't say a word. She fetched a spade and dug a grave for the rabbits and we gave them a decent burial.

Grandfather and Theo organised a whip-round for PeeWee. Everyone in Lyons Terrace and the allotments gave generously and the total came to nearly £200.

"I could make him a new shed," said Grandfather.

"And maybe there'll be enough for a set of secondhand tools," added Theo. I went with them door-to-door while they explained what had happened to PeeWee's shed and allotment. The only two meanies happened to be Mr Khruschev and Mr Porcini. Porky, or Mr Porcini, gave a grand total of 30p while Mr Khruschev, Korky, made a great show of turning out his pocket. "So truly sorry," he said, not sounding at all sorry. "I hev no change, see. What can I say? I vant sooo much to help."

"Well you can give me something later on, after you've been to the bank," Theo said crisply, looking stern and shaking the collecting tin.

"I think Porky and Korky had something to do with the fire," I remarked once we were out of earshot.

"Very likely, fellow-me-lad. But how are we going to prove it, eh?" replied Theo. "And the rabbits? What was the point of that?"

"But why PeeWee's shed? It would have made more sense to burn down Grandfather's. After all, he's their great rival in the veg competition. They want him out of it. They've told everyone they're going to win by hook or by crook."

"Maybe it was a mistake. Maybe they meant to burn down my shed and got the wrong one."

"That's it, Grandfather!" I said, feeling we were on to something. "Porky and Korky could have got someone else to do it and that person got the wrong allotment."

"I still don't see how you're going to prove it," said Theo, not letting go of her point.

Mr Khruschev is quite mad. Everyone knows he is. He says he's a relative of some famous Russian politician. He says the Russian secret police used to be after him so he escaped by tunnelling his way under an electric fence, skating across a frozen lake, hang-gliding over the Ural Mountains and landing on a fishing boat which brought him all the way to Dover. I mean, how gullible does he think we are? He talks like he's James Bond or someone. Actually he's short and tubby with little piggy eyes and bad teeth. He grows his own tobacco and dries it on his shed roof. He calls his shed the *dacha,* which means "country cottage" in Russian. He's always doing something disgusting. He leaves bottles of milk until the milk goes sour and cheesy and then he eats it. He makes pickled cabbage by slinging bits of cut up raw cabbage into a barrel.

You need a clothes peg on your nose if you're anywhere near his allotment in the summer. The smell and the bluebottles buzzing around are horrible. Once he left a big pike that he'd caught in the river out in front of his *dacha*. Of couse it stank after a day or so, and the bluebottles thought it was Christmas. "I leave it for fox," he said, smiling craftily. "When fox come, it eat fish, and then it catch rabbits. Ugh, I hate rabbits."

Of course it had to be him who had killed the rabbits. I knew there had to be a link-up somewhere. The two supernasties of the allotments, Porky and Korky, had to be the villains, but how was I going to prove it?

It was two years ago that Grandfather became obsessed with the idea of winning a lot of money. No, he resisted the Pools because gambling is a sin for Sikhs; he decided to invent a new kind of vegetable. A seed company named Caper and Manger happened to be offering a prize of £5,000 to gardeners who would provide them with seed of a novelty vegetable – something that had never been grown before; something that looked different or tasted different or didn't have to be prepared before being cooked. According to Grandfather, lots of things we take for granted in the shops are the result of cross-breeding different varieties of vegetables and fruit: things like yellow beetroot and blue beans and nectarines, which are a cross between a plum and a peach.

"I want to grow an onion which doesn't make your eyes water when you cut it," he said dreamily.

"Ah, that's because something in it interacts with oxygen in the air and makes sulphuric acid that irritates eyes," said I, showing off.

"So I'll have to find a way of breeding an onion that doesn't have that something in it. It may take me years, but if I win that £5,000 we'll all go for a holiday to my village in India."

Minnie and I have never been to India. Our mum was born in India but she came to live in England with my grandparents when she was fourteen. My dad was born in England, but I don't know much about him because we never see him anymore. I think he lives in Canada.

"Then you'll know what fresh corn bread and spinach from the fields tastes like," said Grandmother enthusiastically. "And freshly churned white butter and sweet buttermilk with an inch of froth on top, and carrot halvah."

"We'll go at *Basant*, the Spring Festival," Grandfather added. "And I'll get my Minnie a little outfit of blossom-yellow silk."

"And we'll fly kites, won't we Grandfather?" said my little sister.

We had this castles-in-the-air conversation every few weeks. It was important for Grandfather to believe that he might one day win his prize money and make his dreams come true.

"I'll buy a good second-hand car, too," he'd

promise us. "A Ford Fiesta with low mileage on it. Your Uncle Harbans knows a reliable dealer in Birmingham."

"Then we'll go to the sea-side again," said Minnie singing. "We haven't been for ages!"

The last time we went to the sea-side was three years ago, when Minnie was five and I was nine. We had a Morris Minor then, but it died of old age. It would be great to go on trips again.

Grandfather had been trying for months to perfect this onion that didn't make you cry. He kept germinating onion seed and cross-pollinating the different varieties with a small sable-hair paintbrush. He planted out seedlings in trays, then pricked them out into tiny little pots and finally planted them in beds in the allotment. He didn't talk about his experiments to anyone except Theo, because she was a jobbing gardener and also his friend.

But somehow word got round that Grandfather was going in for the competition. Once Porky and Korky knew about his plans they decided to compete as well. There had been an awful atmosphere the whole of this growing season. Of course Grandfather was worried that they, rather than he, might win. Without actually telling me to spy on them he dropped enough hints for me to gather that any titbits of news about their plans wouldn't make me the most unpopular person in the world as far as he was concerned.

"They're growing a red cooljet. What's a cooljet?" We tried looking it up in the gardening books. There was nothing like it. The nearest veggie was something called courgette, a kind of small marrow.

Mr Khruschev put his spy training to good use. He rested on his spade a good deal, trying to observe Grandfather's movements. He watched with a beady eye when Grandfather planted out his baby seedlings and tucked them up for a frosty night under a sort of plastic tent. He watched as he mixed special mixtures of plant food for his precious crop. He saw how he carefully squirted insecticide and watered them with soft rainwater taken from the barrel.

There had been a spate of mysterious incidents in the last few months, from the rain-barrel being emptied, the odd seedling pulled up here and there, a dead woodpigeon on the path, to the spud gun affair; and now, the most serious one of all – arson and the vandalism of PeeWee's allotment. I didn't think Porky and Korky could have done it themselves. I had the feeling they had got someone else to burn down the shed. I decided I was going to find out who. I'd keep a look out for anything out of the ordinary and watch them all the time.

Well, I couldn't really watch them all the time because I had to go to school but there were afternoons and evenings. I bought a little notepad and tied a pencil on to it with a rubber band. I'd take notes if I saw anything suspicious. I was quite excited, but I didn't tell anyone about it. Not even my best friend Phil.

Grandfather was working late in the evenings building PeeWee's shed. I was keeping an eye on Korky. Was I imagining it, or was he keeping a low profile? He was still pottering around most days; earthing up potatoes, thinning out carrots, fussing over his seedlings. But he wasn't looking up to see what Grandfather was doing nearly as much. Not leaning on his spade pretending to smoke while he sized up whatever there was to size up. Or was it all an act?

Friday May 14th.

5.35 – P and K talking
in corner of P's allotment.
K seems to be very excited.
His nephew Boris arrives
on his bike with a hosepipe
coiled around his neck like
a boa-constrictor. Now all
three are getting angry.
K is shouting at Boris.

That Sunday evening Mum and I were giving Minnie a cuddle in front of the telly. Grandmother came in and began a monologue: "Harbans says he's taking Jeeti and the children to Disneyland for half term. He offered to take Minnie with them, but I didn't think it was right to leave Baba behind, so I said no thank you. Edna told me that PeeWee's mother is furious with the police. She says they're not bothering to catch the arsonist. She keeps ringing the Police Commissioner but he's always out. Edna says she's going to stop PeeWee from going to the allotment."

"Huh, she'll want him going to knitting classes next," grunted Grandfather. "*Vahe Guru, Vahe Guru!*" He suddenly clapped his hands to his forehead. "Praise God, praise God. What is happening to my brain? I forgot to lock the shed and all my tools are lying there including the power mower."

"I'll go down, Grandfather," I said. "Give me your keys and I'll lock up for you."

Mum looked worried. "It's getting late, child," said Grandfather, "I don't think I should let you go alone."

"It's only a few hundred yards away, Grandfather. Nothing can happen to me."

Grandmother pursed her lips and tucked her *dupatta* behind her ears. Mum relaxed and smiled.

"Go on then, Baba. Take your bike lights and come straight back. Why don't you call Phil to go with you?" But I didn't call him. I had a funny hunch that I might pick up a clue or two about the arson mystery and I wanted to solve it myself.

Trees and bushes were silhouetted against the darkening sky. A little wind played in the hedges. Birds were getting ready to go to bed. I locked my bike to a post outside the allotment gates and looked around. Everyone seemed to have gone home. A thin trickle of smoke from a dying bonfire made a smudge in the air. The air smelled of wood smoke and fresh greenery and cabbages. I wasn't a bit scared. Not really. My bare arms suddenly came out in goosepimples as a shiver ran through me. A branch moved in front of the street lamp making shadows on the path in front. I jumped as a fox quietly padded out from a side lane, looked curiously at me and scuttled away.

Grandfather's allotment was on the far side. It was very quiet except for the rustle of the breeze. All of a sudden I froze, my heart pounding like mad. Someone was talking quietly and the sound was coming from near Grandfather's plot. I tiptoed down a path at the left and, moving as quietly as I could, positioned myself behind his shed, almost in the ditch where I'd found the rabbits. The voices sounded familiar. It was Korky and Boris. Boris sounded as though he was complaining. Korky seemed to be giving him orders in his sergeant-major voice. There was another familiar sound: a match had been struck. Maybe it was nothing; maybe they'd stayed behind to finish off some work and were having a last smoke. But no, cigarettes didn't smell that strong. They'd set fire to something! They were going to burn down *Grandfather's* shed this time!

I heard the crackle of wood and I saw a dart of flame light up the darkness. They were definitely up to no good. I grabbed a sackful of potting compost which was leaning against

the shed wall and charged round to the front. I flung it on the fire which was beginning to blaze on the path between Korky and Grandfather's plots, and very close to Grandfather's territory. I was frightened but also very angry. I heard myself screaming, "Police! Police! Fire! Fire!" as I tore down the central allotment path and headed for the gate and for help against the pyromaniacs.

I came out into the road and I couldn't believe my luck. There was a policeman on a bike, cycling along calmly towards me.

In the short time that I'd run from the scene of the crime, Boris and Korky had stamped out the fire and tidied up the evidence. The path was a bit charred and you could smell the smoke still, but they had scarpered. Nothing could be proved, but P.C. Wallis called round at Mr Khruschev's and made it clear to him that if there was any more funny business at the allotments he would have a lot of explaining to do.

PeeWee's shed got built and Grandfather entered his miracle onion seeds for the competition. But that's another story. And the rabbits? Grandfather Theo and I reckon that Korky and Boris had trapped them for a casserole and then forgotten about the poor creatures and they had suffocated in the fire. After all, Korky had such funny tastes, what with his pickled cabbage and soured milk. I think he and Porky are trying to make beer out of nettles now. There's a new, frightful smell coming from near Korky's shed.

Chapter Two

"There's ghosts in number 97," PeeWee said casually as he was digging up potatoes to take home for supper. They were earlies; smallish, like eggs, smooth as marbles and they sat on the dark rich earth, pale-skinned from having lived underground. I had a picture of PeeWee's mother chopping them into quarters and putting them in front of him for his dinner. Raw. As a treat he might be allowed HP sauce over them. I wondered what he had for pudding. Slugs and snails and puppy dogs' tails, I bet. I didn't like his mum. She'd shouted and waved her broom (her broomstick, more likely) at Phil and me for having a bike race on the pavement.

"What do they look like?" I said to humour him. I was careful to sound perfectly serious.

If there's one thing that makes PeeWee angry it's when people don't take him seriously. He throws wellies when he gets mad.

"I dunno. Haven't seen them. But I've heard them, haven't I."

"What have you heard?" I bent down to pluck a late strawberry from Grandfather's strawberry bed.

"Oh, moanin' and cryin' and howlin'."

I got home, pushed my bike through the back alley and into the garden. Grandfather was in his greenhouse examining his onion seedlings, the ones he's experimenting with for the big £5,000 competition. He looked up briefly and waved. I could see Grandmother through the kitchen window doing something with pots and pans. And there, on the doorstep, lay a dead mouse waiting to welcome me into the house. I looked around for Zebedee. Sure enough, he was at the bottom of the garden,

sitting humped, with his back to me. He was looking with intense longing into the higher reaches of the hedge; he was tracking a bird. I went to consult Grandfather.

"Zebedee's back," (he'd been missing for two days) "and he's brought a present for us."

"Mouse?" Grandfather asked, straightening up. "Nothing you can do about it, Baba. You can't punish him for hunting. He's doing what he's made for. Don't forget he's a wild animal."

Zebedee is not a domestic cat – he's what's called feral. Only last year he was a tiny, soft, cuddly kitten mewing away in the shed of allotment number 97 which used to belong to Mrs Hornstein. When she died, her allotment became so overgrown that no one wanted to take it over. Zebedee must have been abandoned by his mother, who was as wild as they come and well known to the allotment holders. He is now a powerful, wily, charming monster with calculating gooseberry-coloured eyes.

When we found him in Mrs Hornstein's shed we didn't take him home. Grandfather said he wouldn't like it, so we took his meals to him. But one day he decided that we belonged to him and turned up in our garden. He is very independent, even for a cat. Sometimes he sleeps inside the house and sometimes he stays out.

Minnie came into the garden when she saw Zebedee had returned.

"Oh Zebedee, baby, my little sweetheart boy!"

Sweetheart Boy gave my sister a brief glance and returned to his birds. Actually Minnie is his favourite person in our family. She gives him the most cuddles and pieces of Bounty Bar, which he adores. Once when she had done something awful, Mum had punished her by sending her to bed early. Minnie went sobbing to her room and Zebedee bounded after her. A few minutes later Mum went upstairs to see if Minnie was still crying. Zebedee was stretched out on the bed. He looked at her warily. Minnie was under the covers. Mum sat on the bed and was just about to say something like, "I hope you won't do that again, Minnie," when to her astonishment, Zebedee let out a threatening howl and, fixing her with a menacing green stare, put out his front paw and tried to push her off the bed!

When Minnie is angry with me, and Zebedee happens to be around, she will pick him up and talk to him. "You're really my brother, aren't you? Zebedee? Not Baba. He's a bad boy, but you're good, aren't you Zeb, you darling precious sweetheart?"

But Zebedee goes his own way. If he wants

something he just takes it. If he fancies a bit of chicken curry he'll fish it out of a saucepan with his paw. When Grandmother gets angry with him, which she does quite often, he ignores her and walks away. He even knows what to do when he feels thirsty. With a flick of his paw he can tip over a bottle of milk, work the top off with his teeth and lap up the spill.

"PeeWee says there are ghosts in number 97," I said at dinner time.

"PeeWee likes a bit of excitement," Grandfather replied. "Do you know, he told me yesterday that he thought he was going blind. I asked him to take off his spectacles and looked at the lenses. They were perfectly filthy. So I washed them under the tap for him and he was happy again."

"But he says he's been hearing noises coming from Mrs Hornstein's shed."

"It's probably Zebedee living it up," my Mum said.

I told Phil about PeeWee's ghosts. "Let's go and investigate," he said with enthusiasm. Phil loves a mystery. We're going to set up a detective agency when we grow up.

We caught sight of Zebedee sauntering up the path towards number 97. Zebedee has a special kind of saunter, as though he owns wherever he's stepping on. He carried along in his lordly way, tail in the air and, aware that we were following him, skipped nimbly to one side and trotted off in another direction.

The door of Mrs Hornstein's shed was half open. "Look at that," said Phil. On the ground in front of the shed were five or six toilet rolls – ivory, peach, heavenly blue, sunshine, you name the funny colours they name loo-paper, and there was an example of each and every one. Phil giggled.

"The ghosts are collecting bog paper. Or maybe they go to the loo a lot."

Zebedee had appeared on the scene and was giving us a dirty look from where he sat in the middle of the weeds. I pushed the door open cautiously. It creaked in protest. I stepped inside the shed and it was immediately obvious that someone was living there.

Phil and I walked around the shed. It was more than a shed really, more like a summerhouse. It had proper windows and a little porch. There was still an old armchair in which Mrs Hornstein used to sit and play patience on rainy days and a table with an old lace cloth on it. Mrs Hornstein's husband had put up lots of little shelves for her bits and pieces. These were now neatly stacked with tins of baked beans and sardines. Zebedee padded in and *miaowed* in his complaining sort of voice. He looked up at the tins as though he knew the location of the sardines.

On the floor was a rush mat, the kind you take to the beach, and two sausage-shaped rolled-up sleeping bags in one corner. There were a heavy duty torch and several books on the floor. I looked at the books. *Food for Free* was the title of one. Another was about outdoor survival. There were also some comic books, bottled water, plates and cutlery and a tin opener. Two pairs of shoes sat with their toes pointing towards the wall: one looked about a size 10, the other was much smaller.

Zebedee was getting impatient since neither of us was giving him what he was after. He complained a few more times, letting his yowls run back into his throat where they gurgled like water going down a blocked plughole. He nipped my ankle. It was my turn to yowl. "Ow, stop it, Zeb." I bent down to smack his bottom when an unfamiliar voice said, "Chuk chuk chuk chuk. Come here, puss." A strange young man, who had appeared in the doorway, dropped down on his haunches and began to stroke our cat. Behind him was an equally strange-looking girl, or woman – I couldn't make out how old she might have been. They were both wearing faded, sleeveless vests and cut-away dungaree shorts with bits of coloured thread round their wrists and both had long yellow hair pulled back into ponytails.

Neither of them said anything to Phil or me. They just looked at us long and hard as if they were sizing us up. We were so taken aback by their presence that we wouldn't have got any words out of our mouths even if we'd known what to say.

"Nice cat. Is he yours?"

I nodded. The young man had a surprisingly gentle voice and he stroked Zebedee's back lovingly. They had appeared without making a sound and they now came inside on bare feet. I glanced at Phil. He was staring at the girl as if she was from outer space. She was very pretty although her curly blonde hair was tangled and rough and she could have done with a bath or a shower. They both smelled of sweat and living rough. The girl smiled, and said, "Hi, I'm Juliet and this is Mark. Have we been camping in your shed?" She dropped a rucksack on the floor with a thump and reached up to get a sardine tin, which she opened with the tin opener. She put two sardines on a saucer and set it on the floor for Zebedee. Then she took out a loaf of brown bread from her rucksack and started to cut thick slices with a Swiss army penknife.

"Get me a lettuce please, Mark." Mark went out and came back with a fat lettuce dripping black earth from its roots. He twisted the root, tore it off and tossed it out of the door. They had their lunch sitting on the floor and drank from a pint container of milk in turn. Zebedee got a share as well. All this time Phil and I were standing around shifting from foot to

foot, not knowing what to do. Juliet and Mark ignored us. But what annoyed me was the way Zebedee made up to them. He went on Juliet's lap, then he rolled over and let Mark tickle his tummy, purring all the time.

"He's gorgeous. How old is he?" asked Juliet.

I mumbled a reply. Mark opened a book and started reading it, having settled himself comfortably on his sleeping bag.

Juliet looked up at us and said, "Why don't you sit down? What are your names?" We told her and then fell silent.

"I expect you want to know what we're doing here?" she asked. "Well, we've been travelling. We want to wait a while before we go home again, so we're dossing down here. We didn't think any one would mind. Your cat's been around a lot. Did you see the loo paper outside? He keeps bringing us loo rolls.

Have you been missing any at home?"

Come to think of it, Mum and Gran had been going on all week about how quickly we'd been getting through loo paper. So that's where it had been disappearing! Zebedee had been bringing it down to the allotment for his new friends. He must have carried one roll at a time in his teeth – a new kind of present.

"PeeWee thinks you're ghosts," said Phil shyly. I could tell he liked Juliet – he kept staring at her in a gormless way.

"Who's PeeWee?"

I explained. "He's all right. He won't tell anyone about you, but you've got to watch out for Mr Khruschev and Mr Porcini."

"And Mr Little and my dad," added Phil. Mr Little and Phil's dad are on the allotment committee and are very particular about rules.

"We're careful. We don't go out in the daytime; we kept a lookout this afternoon but it's so hot that we reckoned no one would be about straight after lunch so we went to buy some bread and stuff."

"We'd better pick up those loo rolls, otherwise someone will notice and come this way to see what's happening," I said without thinking. I suddenly realised that I didn't want Juliet and Mark to get into trouble. Phil and I went out and threw the toilet rolls into a carrier bag. I felt I should warn Juliet and Mark about lifting lettuces. "They all keep a count of everything and if someone thinks their stuff is being nicked they'll do everything they can to find out what's going on."

Phil and I went home in a state of great excitement. We had a secret no one knew about and we were going to do our best to see that no one found out about Juliet and Mark. But someone did, and that someone was Minnie.

We'd been going to visit our new friends every day for about a week. Usually we just sat and chatted with them. Sometimes we played cards and once or twice we fetched things for them from the shops. We didn't want Mr Patel getting suspicious about our shopping because it was so different from what we would get for our mums, so we went to the other end of town where nobody knew us. Juliet and Mark kept a low profile. They didn't sing or talk above a whisper, in case PeeWee came hunting for ghosts. And I told Mum that Zebedee had been stealing the toilet rolls so she should hide them inside a cupboard. Otherwise he would have carried on doing it and someone might have noticed sooner or later, even though Mrs Hornstein's shed was over the far side where people didn't normally come.

But Zebedee continued to be unfaithful and more or less stayed away from our house.

"He's got the call of the wild," said Phil. "He remembers where he was born. Cats are very sensitive. They've got psychiatrists for them in the States. My aunt told me." Phil's aunt lives in America so that makes him an expert on anything to do with that country.

But Minnie wasn't happy that Zebedee had abandoned her. She knew he was living in the allotment, though I hadn't said exactly where. She kept pestering me to show her, and I said I'd take her there, but whenever she wanted to be taken I'd invent an excuse.

One day Phil and I set off to see Juliet and Mark and, without our knowing it, Minnie decided to follow us. Of course she didn't know about those two, but she guessed correctly that we were going to the allotments. She must have thought that once we were there she would get me to take her to Zebedee's hideout. She managed to slip out without Grandmother noticing and then she followed us. The allotments are very near Lyons Terrace, only a few hundred yards behind our house. We had just got to Mrs Hornstein's shed when we heard her calling behind us, "Baba, Phil, wait for me," and she ran up to us.

I looked around. A few people were working on their plots, but they were all far away. Zebedee, hearing Minnie's voice, sidled out of the shed.

"Oh, *there* he is, my darling boy!" cried Minnie. Zebedee turned tail and bolted back inside. Minnie ran after him.

"You can't go in there," I said barring her way, but she pushed past me and was inside before I could stop her. We followed, Phil shrugging his shoulders helplessly.

"Oh!" said Minnie. "Hello ..." and turned to us, not knowing what to do.

Juliet and Mark were sitting on the floor. Mark was reading and Juliet was writing in her diary. One of the nicest things about them both was that they never seemed to mind about anything. I'd never once seen them rattled. Mark gave Minnie a friendly smile.

"Have a biscuit," he said.

Minnie didn't need to be told that Mark and Juliet were a secret. She may be only eight, but she has loads of sense. She liked the idea of keeping something as important as that from the grownups. But our secret didn't stay hidden for very long after that.

Grandfather had been talking about getting a second allotment for himself, and a few days later he announced that he was thinking of taking over Mrs Hornstein's plot.

"It's a terrible idea, Grandfather," I told him. "It's about as far as you can get from the water tap."

"Oh, that won't be a problem. I've thought about it already and the committee have said I can run a hosepipe to number 97."

I ran as fast as I could to the shed and told Juliet and Mark that Grandfather was on his way over to inspect the shed and start digging the ground.

"We'll have to meet your grandfather, then. We can't move out in five minutes flat," Mark said casually. "We'll just take a chance. Maybe he'll like us."

He did like them. Mark and Juliet had spent six months travelling in India and had been to lots of places which Grandfather knew. They chatted for absolutely ages and Juliet brewed him some tea on her primus stove. She boiled tea leaves and water and milk and sugar together and handed him a mug.

"It's like the tea you get at wayside stops

when you travel by bus, isn't it?"

"That's right. Takes me back to old times, it does," said Grandfather.

After they had talked for a little while more, he asked Mark and Juliet what their plans were. They shrugged. "We haven't any."

"But you've got A-levels. You should be think of training for jobs."

Mark and Juliet didn't think that was important.

"You won't be able to stay here much longer. Once I take over the plot I'll have to let the committee know you're here. I couldn't break the rules."

"That's OK, Mr Singh. Don't worry about us. We'll just move on."

Grandfather thought for a moment. "You must come and have a meal with us at home before you go. Come tomorrow and my wife will make *chapattis* for you."

Grandmother was appalled. "Who is this boy and girl? Why don't their parents help them? Jarnail Singhji," She said addressing Grandfather, "Balwinder should not have been spending his afternoons with these people. They could be drug addicts or alcoholics. Now you expect me to cook *chapattis* for them. *Vahe Guru*, *Vahe Guru*, that I should live to see this. It's a scandal you are bringing hippies into our home."

Grandfather and I tried to calm her down. Minnie tried too.

"They've been so kind to Zebedee, Grandmother. They gave him a whole tin of sardines every day."

But that was no way to soothe her. "That cat! I've always said he will send me to an early end! The trouble he causes. And you say he's been stealing toilet rolls! What next? I think he's more of a nuisance every day. We should give him away!" At which point Minnie burst into tears. Grandmother finally managed to stop ranting and began preparing supper with her *dupatta* tucked firmly behind her ears and her lips pursed up very tightly.

It was a really nice evening in the end. Juliet turned up wearing a *shalwar kameez*. She told Grandmother that she had worn it every day in India and that it was the most beautiful and comfortable garment in the world, and that pleased Grandmother since she wears one herself. Juliet and Mark ate in the Indian way, with their fingers, and managed to let it be known that they didn't drink. By now Grandmother was more relaxed. It was difficult not to like them.

After dinner Grandfather walked back with them to the shed where they were going to spend their last night. He was gone for ages. Phil went home and I went to bed. Next

morning Grandfather asked me to come and give him a hand on his new allotment and I was glad to say yes because it would give me the chance of seeing Juliet and Mark for the last time.

But they had already gone. There was an envelope addressed to Mr Singh stuck in the door frame. Grandfather opened it and as he read a smile appeared on his face.

"Where've they gone, Grandfather? What does it say?"

He handed the letter to me to read.

"Dear Mr Singh,

It's dawn and we want to be on the road before the early-birds get to their allotments. We thought about what you said last night and you may have a point. We've decided to go back home and look up our parents and see how things stand. Mark and I should start making plans for what we want to do. I want to see if I can get a place at college and train to be a teacher.

We both want to thank you for everything you've done for us. It was great having that time to think in your allotment shed. Please thank Phil and Baba and Minnie for their friendship, and your daughter and wife for the wonderful meal last night. We'll be in touch and let you know what happens to us.

    With best wishes,

    Mark and Juliet

P.S. There's a tin of sardines for Zebedee on the shelf. Please give him a cuddle from us.

I looked at Grandfather. He was still smiling. "They're going to be all right," he said. "Come on, there's a lot of work to do." We've started to dig the allotment.

Chapter Three

Baba's Brainwave

Getting Grandfather's new allotment cleaned up was backbreaking work. We were at it for over a week and PeeWee gave us a hand as well. There were all the surface weeds to be pulled out. Then we dug deep and turned the earth over.

"Leave the grass and weeds on top. The sun will dry them up," Grandfather told me.

I saw Mr Porcini making his way towards us.

"Hello, hello!" he cried with a false-sounding jollity. "What are we up to now?"

"Clearing the weeds first and then I'll see," replied Grandfather.

PeeWee turned away muttering to himself. He had not spoken to Mr Porcini or Mr Khruschev for weeks. His mother, old Ma Pollit, had had her little revenge, though. Early one morning she'd been to the allotments collecting a bucketful of snails which she'd gleefully scattered all over Porky and Korky's salad greens. All this was meant to be a dark secret, but PeeWee had whispered it to Grandfather.

"She had a go at their marrows and leeks too, Mr Singh," he confided. Marrow-slashing was the one way of making sure someone's prize entry didn't stand a chance in the allotment show. A scratch on the skin of a marrow becomes an ugly-looking scar which ruins its appearance. If you think crime and vandalism is something new, you're wrong. Assaults on marrows have been going on since the dawn of time – or since vegetable-growing competitions and shows started, anyway.

"And then she poured bleach all over Korky's tomato plants," continued PeeWee.

"I don't want to know," Grandfather said firmly, but I was beside myself. I laughed like a drain. I didn't like Ma Pollit one little bit, but she had given those two what they deserved.

"Well, I'd better be off. Just came to offer our – that is, Mr Khruschev's and my – congratulations. All the best then," and Mr Porcini made his way back to his own plot.

Grandfather had bagged first prize for the biggest marrow and the best runner beans in the annual allotment show. The marrow was a huge, stripey monster which could have fed my whole class at school. The runner beans were a beautiful, even shade of pale green and as straight as soldiers. He'd got two red and white rosettes and a bottle of brandy which he'd given to Mr Tomkins next door.

"Can't imagine why you want another allotment," grumbled Grandmother. "We have more than enough cabbages and tomatoes and beans and spinach. Why do you want to make more work for yourself? You need to put up your feet and stay at home. What are you going to grow that you need more of? As it is you give away half your produce. You shouldn't think of yourself as a charity. If people want fresh vegetables they ought to get their own allotments. Imagine relying on an old man like you to keep them in food ..." She was away.

Grandfather cleared his throat mildly. "Actually, I was thinking of growing flowers for a change," he said.

"Well, that would be nice. But do you need a whole allotment for them? Wouldn't half an allotment be enough?"

"I've been thinking, Bebeji; you know how much money the *gurdwara* committee spends on flowers every week. It's a shame it should cost so much to run a religious service. We could spend that money on some good cause, like outings for old people. If I grow the flowers for the *gurdwara* and charge them very little I could do the same for the Ramakrishna Temple and All Saints Church."

"And maybe the temple and All Saints would contribute something in return to the outings for old people," Grandmother said thoughtfully. "Jarnail Singhji, not only are you a very clever person but you are also a good man."

Grandfather beamed. It was rare for Grandmother to pay a compliment.

Phil and I were starting to get a little bored. It was too hot to do much. We went ice-skating and swimming and fishing. I read three books. Phil read ten comics. I helped to dig and tidy up the shed at number 97. Meanwhile Grandfather was getting all kinds of advice about his flower-growing scheme.

"Stick to bulbs and perennials," advised Phil's dad.

"Why don't you try those lovely old-fashioned annuals?" someone else suggested.

Grandfather enjoyed himself looking at various seed-merchants' catalogues, making ticks in the margin.

"The most important flower for our *gurdwara* service is marigold. Those big, pom-pom yellow and orange ones," Grandmother insisted.

"Phew, they smell awful," my mum said, wrinkling her nose.

"And roses, Jarnail Singhji. Don't forget roses. Dark red and pink roses," Grandmother went on. "Gladioli would look pretty on the platform, next to the Holy Book, the *Granth Sahib*."

Grandfather went on marking, his spectacles slipping off his nose. He added up all his sums on the back of an envelope, and wiped his forehead disbelievingly.

"Do you know, Bebeji, how much these seeds and bulbs are going to cost?" he asked Grandmother. "Over £180. I don't know if I can afford to start this little scheme." He looked very dejected.

That was when I had a brainwave. I would help Grandfather get together the money he needed to buy all his bulbs and seeds. I only had the beginnings of an idea in my head. This summer the temperature had been high for over two weeks and every day the weatherman forecast more hot sun and cloudless skies. I talked it over with Phil.

"Let's set up a refreshment stall near the allotment gates. Cold home-made lemonade, Grandmother's special *nimboopani* recipe, slices of watermelon, biscuits or home-made cake. When people see all these yummy things all laid out on a table, they'll want to try them."

We did some calculations. If we charged

10p a glass of lemonade, we could make a profit of 5p a glass. We'd need to sell thirty glasses to the allotment holders to make £1.50 profit a day and that was only on drinks. We could make more on food. In ten days we might earn £50.

We got permission from Phil's dad and from Mr Little. They're both big shots on the Allotment Committee. "As long as you don't obstruct the entrance, or any of the access routes," Mr Little said pompously looking at us belligerently through his glasses.

Phil and I spent a lot of time doing sums and working out what his dad called "profit margins." We calculated the cost of buying lemons and sugar and flour and margarine and working out what people would pay for a serving of lemonade and piece of cake or a biscuit.

"It's not the true cost, see. We haven't

allowed for labour, that's the time you and I and your granny'll spend making all this stuff to sell. We haven't allowed for fuel, that's the cost of gas which your granny will use when she bakes. So actually it's going to cost a lot more than 25p for a piece of cake, but we can't charge any more because it'll be too expensive to buy."

It was a bit depressing when you saw it like that. Still, we were on holiday and our time was free; and Grandmother liked cooking anyway and she was always using the stove and the oven, so a tray of biscuits could cook at the same time as something else.

Phil became very business-like and organised.

"We'll buy from whoever gives us the best deal," he said firmly. "Let's ask around the shops." So we set off for town armed with a shopping list to do some comparisons. Having trailed around various shops, it was obvious that the supermarkets were going to be the cheapest. We sat on a bench in the shopping centre and did some sums.

"Don't forget the bus fare to town," said Phil. "That's going to add on quite a bit." In the end we decided to pay a visit to Lovely Department Store, to see if Mr Patel could match the supermarket prices.

Lovely Department Store was only a street away from Lyons Terrace. Minnie and I liked going there because Mr Patel always gave us a treat. He was a friend of Grandfather's. Once Grandfather had frightened burglars away from the Patel's house and Mr and Mrs Patel had never forgotten that. Sometimes Grandfather minded the shop for Mr Patel.

It was a small corner shop which sold everything from newspapers to knitting needles to onion *bhajis.* Grandmother liked shopping there because the Patels were so friendly and Mum liked it because it was open when she got back late from the hospital.

"Let me see, let me see," said Mr Patel, taking our list. He was a jolly man with a round, bald head which twinkled in the light. He pushed his spectacles up to his forehead and peered at it. Usually people put on their specs when they have to read something but it was the other way round for Mr Patel.

"How much will all this cost in the supermarket?" he asked shrewdly. We told him.

"No problem, no problem." Mr Patel always repeated his sentences. "I can match this cent for cent. What's more I can give you a discount. Look, every week I have lemons left over from the week before. They don't look so fresh, but there's still a lot of juice inside them. If you soak them in hot water first you get double the amount of juice. Free tip! No extra charge for my secrets!"

Phil nudged me in the ribs. "We'll think it over. Come on, Balwinder" he said, addressing me formally, and pulled me outside.

"What did you do that for? He'll think we're rude. Anyway it looks like the cheapest quote we've got so far."

"Yes, but that's not how you do business. You've always got to say, 'I'll think it over'." Phil grinned. "It's a really good deal. And we won't have to travel to town to buy our stuff each week."

Considering we only had two weeks left of the holidays it wouldn't have broken the bank to take two return trips by bus into town. But Phil was completely into being a big tycoon now. Costs, profits, losses. We gave our order to Mr Patel.

Three days later we were in business. Grandfather helped us set up a table under a tree. We made two litres of lemonade and four dozen biscuits with Gran's help. Phil's mother lent us some glasses and a bucket and tea towels for washing up and Minnie wrote out price labels. I propped them up beside the food and drink. "10p a glass" and "10p each" for the biscuits (we decided that 25p was too ambitious).

We were all ready by ten o'clock.

In the morning it was the pensioners and people who were out of work who came to their allotments. We counted twenty and it was funny how they seemed to ignore our stall like they hadn't really seen us. Some said "Hello," but most just went on without any comment. But it was hotter that day than it had ever been and an hour or so later people started to come and buy our drinks.

"This is really good."

"Well done, lads."

"Oh, I could drink a bucket of this stuff," were some of the things were heard. The biscuits went down well, too. In the afternoon we got more customers as people came by after work. We had to go home to get more lemonade at around five o'clock. Of course we had a break at lunch time, but we had clocked up about eight hours altogether at the end of our first day. We took home nearly ten pounds.

The next day was just as good, but the day after that it rained so we didn't bother going.

Word started to spread about our stall. Phil's mother told all her friends and they stopped for a drink and a biscuit on their way home from the shops or work. Even Ma Pollit came to see what we were up to. She bought a biscuit and chewed on it as if it might bite her. Then she had a drink.

"There ain't enough sugar in this," she said in her croaky voice.

Phil looked at me. She was a scary old thing.

"Would you like some extra, Mrs Pollit?" asked Phil politely.

She glared at him. "Should have put in enough in the first place, shouldn't you? You can't charge fancy prices if it ain't sweet enough." She put down her glass with a thump and walked off. Phil called after her, "That's 10p Mrs Pollit." She turned back with a scowl on her face and paid up, but went off talking to herself.

I hadn't said anything to Grandfather about what we were going to do with the money we earned so it became very difficult when he turned out to be our best customer. He seemed to get thirsty every twenty minutes or so and he insisted on paying us.

"This is hopeless," I told Phil. "What's the point of taking his money and then giving it back to him? First he spends his own money and then we give it back to him and tell him it's for his seed and bulbs. It doesn't make sense, does it?"

"There's going to be a thunderstorm today. The weather forecast said so," Grandfather warned me at breakfast. "Might be a bit dangerous under that tree."

"We'll pack up as soon as we hear thunder," I said. In fact the thunderstorm didn't come that day but we got caught in the middle of another kind of storm.

First of all Old Ma Pollit appeared carrying a basket on her arm. She took out a bottle with some greyish-looking liquid in it and plonked it on our table.

"This is beautiful home-made elderflower cordial," she announced and took two more bottles from her basket. "It's a pound a bottle.

Beautiful stuff. You can't find it in the shops. Old family secret it is. You'll have people queuing up to buy it."

Phil looked at me helplessly. She put her face close to his.

"You can have 5p for each bottle you sell," Ma Pollit said generously and shuffled off to see what PeeWee was up to. Phil shrugged and made a face.

Minutes after she had gone there was a sound of loud voices at the entrance to the allotments and the squeal of bike brakes. Three teenagers swaggered in. One of them was Korky's nephew, Boris. He was wearing a baseball hat back to front and swinging a bicycle chain in one hand.

"Oh, oh, I smell trouble," Phil whispered. The three hulks came and stood in front of us. They stared at Phil and then at me.

"What are you waiting for? Three of those," a hulk said, pointing at the lemonade.

"Yeah, we're thirsty. Get on with it," said another hulk.

Phil squared his jaw. "That's 30p," he said fearlessly, holding out his hand for the money. Boris bared his teeth in what he supposed was a sinister way. I had a sudden urge to laugh, but I controlled myself. The biggest hulk grabbed a glass and poured himself a drink. The other was about to help himself when Phil put his hand over the jug.

"Payment first." He was nearly squeaking with nervousness. Boris leaned over.

"Go on, make my day, punk," he growled, imitating Clint Eastwood.

The other two sniggered. I was starting to get angry and wondering if I should call Grandfather for help, when who should walk up but Grandfather himself. He was a good six inches taller than the teenagers. I could tell that he had taken in the situation in no time at all.

"Hello, Boris. Are you enjoying your holidays? And who are these two young men? Are you all at the same school?" Grandfather put 10p on the table and thanked Phil as he handed him a glass of lemonade. At this point the hulk who had downed our lemonade took some change out of his pocket and put a coin on the table, not daring to look either of us in the face.

Grandfather's friend, Theo, arrived on her bike. She gulped down a lemonade.

"What's this?" she pointed squeamishly to the bottles of elderflower cordial. "Not Mrs Pollit's brew?" I nodded.

"Don't touch it, it's pure poison."

Phil look thoroughly alarmed. He is a very law-abiding person, just like his dad.

"No, I didn't mean that literally," Theo said, noticing his expression. "It tastes foul, because she probably made it ten years ago. I'm sure it's fermented and become alcohol, so you'd be breaking the licensing laws," she said, teasing Phil.

In the general chit-chat under the tree, Boris and his pals slithered away, looking rather sheepish.

"All right boys?" asked Grandfather. We both nodded. He picked up Mrs Pollit's bottles. "I'll get rid of these. Don't worry, I'll give her three pounds and we'll pretend they've been sold."

"You see!" I said to Phil after Grandfather had gone. "It's hopeless."

In the end we made a profit of £37. It would have been more but we got washed out. The rain poured down every day until the day before the holidays ended. But the most brilliant thing happened on the Saturday before school started. We were having breakfast, all of us, because it was Mum's day off, when the phone went.

"It's for you, Dad," said Mum, handing the receiver to Grandfather.

"Yes," said Grandfather "Yes, it is. Really? Oh that's wonderful." He turned to us beaming all over. "Right, I'll be pleased to come. May I bring my family? Thank you. Good, look forward to it. Goodbye." He hung up. He was absolutely bursting with excitement.

"You'll never guess what's happened!"

Yes, Grandfather had won the competition for the most original vegetable with his tearless onion! There was a big presentation in London and we all went with him to celebrate his win. Everyone was happy that Grandfather had won. All the allotment owners sent him a card and so did all our neighbours in Lyons Terrace.

"You know, Grandfather, isn't it funny that we live in Lyons Terrace and our surname means 'lion' in Punjabi?" Minnie remarked.

"That's right, Singh means 'lion'. What a strange thing, to be sure," chuckled Grandfather. He was busy looking at brochures, only this time they were for holidays in India. Grandmother stirred something on the stove.

"Jarnail Singhji, I think our Harbans is thinking of taking Jeeti and the children to India as well. He wants to show them the Golden Temple in Amritsar and the Taj Mahal in Agra. Should we all go together on the same flight? I did mention it to Harbans, but he didn't think it would be such a good idea in case the plane crashed and then the whole family would be wiped out. Perhaps the children and I could travel on one flight and you could go with the others ..." Grandmother was away on one of her monologues.

"Grandfather," I said, sitting next to him. "You know that £37 we collected for your seeds and bulbs? What shall we do with it?" I hoped he'd say something like, "Oh, why don't you and Phil and Minnie blow it on McDonalds, sweets and the movies?"

Instead he said, "There is the old people's outing fund at the *gurdwara*." And then seeing my face he added, "Give them half and you and Minnie and Phil share the rest between you."

I tell you, my grandfather is the best.